play forever on video and

Published by Ladybird Books Ltd.
A Penguin Company
Penguin Books Ltd., 80 Strand, London WC2R 0RL
Penguin Books Australia Ltd., Camberwell, Victoria, Australia
Penguin Books (NZ) Ltd., Private Bag 102902, NSMC, Auckland,
New Zealand
LADYBIRD and the device of a ladybird
are trademarks of Ladybird Books, Ltd.
11 13 15 17 19 20 18 16 14 12
Printed in Italy

WALT DISNEY'S

CLASSIC

101 DALMATIANS

Ladybird

Roger Radcliff was a musician. He lived in a little flat in London with Pongo, his pet Dalmatian dog.

One day, Roger got married. His
lovely new wife was called Anita –
and she had a beautiful lady
Dalmatian called Perdita.

Soon, Perdita was expecting her first litter of puppies. Life seemed perfect until one day, an old friend of Anita's, Cruella De Vil, came to visit. Perdita and Pongo were frightened of her.

"Where are the puppies?" Cruella demanded.

"They're not expected for another three weeks," Anita replied.

"You *must* let me know when they arrive. I just *adore* Dalmatian puppies – their coats are *so* beautiful." And with that, Cruella swept out of the house in a flurry.

Three weeks later, Perdita and Pongo became the proud parents of fifteen puppies. Roger, Anita and Nanny, the housekeeper, were delighted.

The very next day, Cruella returned.
"Fifteen puppies!" she cried,
excitedly. "I'll buy *all* of them."

"Oh no, you won't," said Roger,
"they're *not* for sale."

"You fools! You'll be sorry!" Cruella
cried, storming out of the house.

One night soon after, Cruella's
henchmen, Horace and Jasper Badun,
lay in wait to dognap the puppies.
They sat in their van and waited for
Roger and Anita to take Perdita and
Pongo for their evening walk.

Once the coast was clear, the Baduns
forced their way into the house.
When Nanny tried to stop them, the
Baduns locked her in a broom
cupboard.

By the time Nanny managed to
escape, the Baduns were gone – and
so were the puppies!

The police immediately launched an
investigation, but as the days went
by, the puppies were still not found.

At last, Pongo said to Perdita, "The humans aren't getting anywhere. We'll have to find the puppies ourselves."

Pongo decided to try the Twilight Bark. This was the quickest way for dogs to send and receive news across the country.

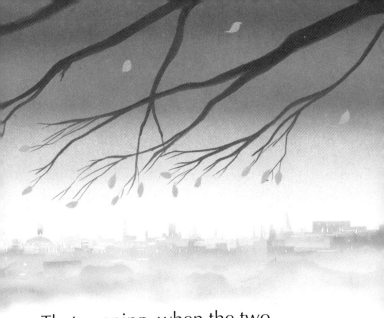

That evening, when the two
Dalmatians were taken for their
walk, Pongo barked the alert – three
loud barks and a howl – from the top
of Primrose Hill.

After a moment an answering bark
was heard. "It's the Great Dane at
Hampstead!" Pongo said to Perdita,
and he barked out his message.

Danny the Great Dane was very
surprised by the message. "Fifteen
Dalmatian puppies have been
stolen!" he told a terrier friend. "The
humans haven't been able to find
them, so it's up to us to send out an
all-dog alert with the Twilight Bark."

Danny's big deep voice began to
send the news all over London…

Two mongrels heard the alert. One said, "I think we should let the rest of the country know."

And so, within the hour, word had spread north, south, east and west – all over England.

Before too long, the Twilight Bark reached an old sheepdog called Colonel, who lived on a farm.

Colonel's friends – a horse named Captain and a cat named Tibs – listened too. They were all very surprised to hear that fifteen puppies had been stolen!

"That's funny," Tibs said to Captain and Colonel. "I heard puppies barking over at the old De Vil house last night."

"But no one lives there now," said Colonel. "We must go and see what's going on."

So Colonel and Tibs went quietly up to the house and peered through a broken window.

Inside the house, Horace and Jasper Badun were eating supper and relaxing in front of the television.

All round the room there were puppies. Not fifteen – nor even fifty – but *ninety-nine* of them!

Colonel quickly returned to
Captain's stable and loudly barked
the good news. Within no time at all,
the Twilight Bark sent the message
all the way back to London that the
puppies had been found.

It finally reached the ears of Perdita
and Pongo. They set off across the
snowy countryside as fast as they
could to rescue their puppies.

Meanwhile, Sergeant Tibs was keeping watch on the house. When he saw Cruella drive up to the front door, he went to the broken window to hear what was happening.

Cruella was ordering the Baduns to
kill the puppies! "I want their skins
for fur coats!" she cried. "I'll be back
first thing in the morning." And with
that warning she left.

Tibs was horrified. Fur coats from
puppy skins! What a terrible thought.

There wasn't a moment to lose. As soon as the Baduns began watching television again, Tibs crept through the broken window and whispered to the nearest puppy, "Tell everyone they must escape. Cruella is after your coats!"

When all the puppies had been alerted, Tibs led them out of the room and up the stairs to find a hiding place.

As soon as the Baduns discovered
that the puppies had gone, they
searched all over the house and
eventually headed up the stairs.

The puppies were cowering in a corner of a bedroom. Tibs was in front ready to protect them from the Baduns.

Meanwhile, Colonel had met up with Perdita and Pongo and led them to the De Vil house. They arrived just in the nick of time and quickly bounded into action.

Perdita attacked Horace Badun,
while Pongo tore at Jasper Badun's
trousers.

Under cover of the fight, Tibs led the
puppies out of the house to the
safety of Captain's stable.

Leaving the Baduns in a heap on the floor, Perdita and Pongo dashed after the puppies.

"Are our fifteen all here?" asked Perdita, anxiously.

"Your fifteen and a few more," replied Captain. "There are *ninety-nine*!"

"*Ninety-nine!*" said Pongo, astonished. "Whatever did Cruella want with *ninety-nine* puppies?"

There was silence for a moment, then one little puppy said, "She was going to make fur coats out of us."

Perdita and Pongo looked at each other in horror. They had never heard of anything so evil.

"We'll just have to take them *all* back to London with us," said Perdita. "I'm sure Roger and Anita will look after them."

Perdita, Pongo and the puppies set
off back to London, leaving a trail of
pawprints in the snow.

Cruella, who had returned for the
puppies' coats, quickly spotted the
pawprints – and the chase began…

Eventually, after trudging across the countryside, Perdita and Pongo led the tired puppies to the shelter of a blacksmiths' shop. Cruella and the Baduns were still on their trail.

Suddenly, Pongo had an idea. He made the puppies roll in some soot until they all looked like black Labradors.

37

Under the cover of their disguise, the puppies climbed into a van that was going to London. But falling snow flakes began to wash away the soot.

Cruella saw white patches appearing on the puppies' coats and realised that she had been tricked. "After them!" she shouted to the Baduns.

Pongo just had time to leap on to the
tailboard as the van sped off – with
Cruella and the Baduns right behind.

Cruella was determined to force the van off the road. But as she banged into the side of it, her car skidded out of control and hurtled down a steep hill into a snowdrift.

Then the Baduns' van crashed into
the back of Cruella's car – and they
all ended up in a large pile of
wreckage!

Back in London and home at last, Roger, Anita and Nanny hugged the tired puppies. Then Nanny said, "Have you noticed that there seems to be a lot more of them?"

Roger started to count. "Fourteen – sixty-two – ninety-four – and five over there. That's a hundred and one Dalmatians counting Perdita and Pongo!"

"Whatever are we going to do with them all?" asked Anita.

"Why, keep them of course," said Roger. "We'll buy a big house and have a Dalmatian Plantation!"

And that's exactly what they did!

Yours
to own
on Disney
DVD

WALT DISNEY
CLASSICS

Magical stories to